TURKEY ON THE LOOSE!

by Sylvie Wickstrom

Dial Books for Young Readers New York

Published by Dial Books for Young Readers
A Division of Penguin Books USA Inc.
375 Hudson Street
New York, New York 10014

Printed in Hong Kong by South China Printing Company (1988) Limited
First Edition
W
10 9 8 7 6 5 4 3 2 1
Library of Congress Cataloging in Publication Data
Wickstrom, Sylvie.
Turkey on the loose! / by Sylvie Wickstrom.
p.   cm.
Summary: A turkey gets loose in an apartment house
and creates havoc.
ISBN 0-8037-0818-1.—ISBN 0-8037-0820-3 (lib. bdg.)
1. Turkeys—Fiction. 2. Apartment houses—Fiction.
I. Title.   PZ7.W6295Tu 1990
[E]—dc20   89-26056   CIP   AC

The art for each picture consists of a pencil and watercolor painting,
which is scanner-separated and reproduced in full color.

For my Uncle Salomon

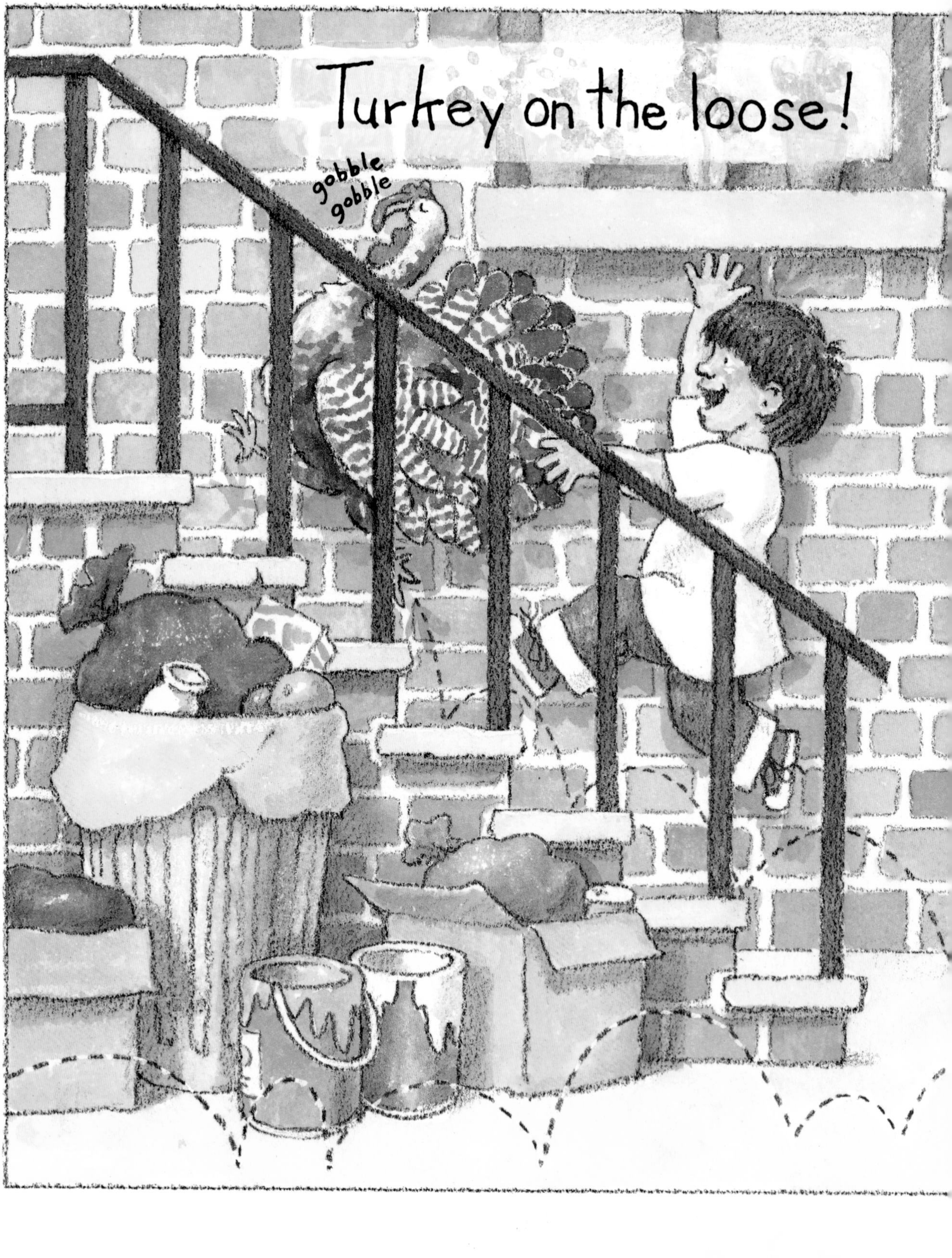
Turkey on the loose!
gobble gobble

gobble

bonk!

Excuse us, Turkey on the loose!